This book belongs to

....

LADYBIRD BOOKS

UK | USA | Canada | Ireland | Australia | India | New Zealand | South Africa

Ladybird Books is part of the Penguin Random House group of companies
whose addresses can be found at global.penguinrandomhouse.com.

www.penguin.co.uk   www.puffin.co.uk   www.ladybird.co.uk

Penguin
Random House
UK

First published 2020
001

eOne   ASTLEY · BAKER · DAVIES

Printed in China

A CIP catalogue record for this book is available from the British Library

ISBN: 978-0-241-41224-4

All correspondence to:
Ladybird Books
Penguin Random House Children's
One Embassy Gardens, 8 Viaduct Gardens, London SW11 7BW

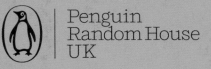

George's Tractor

Peppa and George were spending the day at Granny and Grandpa Pig's house.
"We're very glad you're here," said Grandpa Pig.
"You can help us harvest the vegetables."

"Hooray!" cheered Peppa and George, jumping up and down. "Grandpa, what does 'harvest the vegetables' mean?" asked Peppa.

"Ho! Ho!" Grandpa Pig chuckled. "When we harvest the vegetables, it means we pick them so we can eat them."
"Oooh," said Peppa. "Yummy!"
"Yummy!" cried George, rubbing his tummy.

Yummy!

"Let's go and harvest," said Granny Pig. "It's a good job we've got our boots on. It's very muddy out here."

Peppa and George had lots of fun helping Granny and Grandpa Pig harvest their vegetables. Soon, there were huge piles of vegetables all around them.
"What a big harvest, Grandpa!" gasped Peppa.

"Yes, it is, Peppa," replied Grandpa Pig. "The biggest
we've had in a long time. Isn't that right, Granny Pig?
Er, Granny Pig . . . where are you?"
Peppa, George and Grandpa Pig looked around.
They couldn't see Granny Pig anywhere . . .

"Over here!" shouted Granny Pig, poking her head out from a tall pile of carrots.

"Ahhh, there you are," said Grandpa Pig, smiling.

"Granny!" said Peppa. "You look a bit . . . carroty!"
George giggled. "Hee! Hee! Gangy-ig!"

"Next, we need to get all these vegetables into those crates over there," said Grandpa Pig, pointing to the other side of the garden.

"All the vegetables, Grandpa?" asked Peppa.
"Yes," replied Grandpa Pig. "Every single one!"
Everyone looked at the enormous piles of vegetables . . .
"Oh," said Peppa.

Peppa, Granny Pig and
Grandpa Pig began carrying
the vegetables over to the crates.
The crates were far away.
Peppa looked around.
"Where's George . . . ?"

"BRUM! BRUM! Trac-tor!" cried George.
He loaded up his toy tractor's trailer with lots
of vegetables and moved them over to the crates.
"That's very clever, George," said Granny Pig.
"Your tractor will make this **much** easier!"

BRUM!
BRUM!

Everyone helped George load and unload his tractor.
"That's everything!" said Grandpa Pig. "Thank you
for your help, Farmer George and Farmer Peppa."
"BRUM! BRUM! Trac-tor!" said George.

"What are we going to do with all the vegetables now, Grandpa?" asked Peppa. "We can't eat them all . . . can we?"
"No, Peppa, I don't think we can eat them all!" replied Grandpa Pig.

"I know a special place we can take them," said Granny Pig. "It's somewhere you and George will enjoy visiting."
"Yippee!" cried Peppa and George.

Granny and Grandpa Pig took Peppa and George to a farmers' market.

"At a farmers' market, farmers and growers sell their fruits and vegetables," Granny Pig explained.

BRUM! BRUM!

George was excited to see all the big tractors.
"BRUM! BRUM! TRAC-TOR!" he shouted.

George spotted an enormous tractor and pointed. "BRUM! BRUM! BIG trac-tor!"
"Wow! I think that's the biggest tractor I've ever seen, George," said Granny Pig.

While George and Granny Pig went to see the big tractor, Grandpa Pig and Peppa started setting up a stall for their vegetables.

Suddenly, they heard a loud rumbling noise.
BRUM! BRUM! It was George on Mrs Badger's tractor,
carrying all the crates of vegetables!

"WOW!" gasped Peppa. "George is on a **real** tractor!"
"BIG trac-tor!" cried George, as everybody unloaded the crates.
"Thank you, Farmer George!" said Grandpa Pig. "Now our
vegetable stall is ready."

BRUM!
BRUM!

Farmer Peppa and Farmer George had lots of fun selling the vegetables. "Rebecca!" cried Peppa, spotting Rebecca Rabbit. "Come and buy some of our vegetables."

"Oooh, what a lot of lovely carrots," said Mummy Rabbit. "How did you get them all here?"
"BRUM! BRUM! BIG trac-tor!" said George.
"I see," said Mummy Rabbit. "I would like to buy **all** your carrots, please!"

There were lots of customers at the farmers' market.
Farmer Peppa, Farmer George, Granny and Grandpa Pig
were very busy selling their vegetables.

"Hello, Farmer Peppa and Farmer George," said Daddy Pig.
"Hello, Daddy," said Peppa. "What would you like?"
"Erm . . ." said Daddy Pig, looking at the empty stall.
"Oh," said Peppa. "We don't have anything left."

"Never mind," said Mummy Pig.
"It's time to go home now. What
would you like for supper?"
"Carrots, please!" said Peppa.

"As you've sold all yours, we'll have to get some from the shop," said Mummy Pig. "But how will we get there?"

"BRUM! BRUM! Trac-tor!" cried George.

George loved the farmers' market, but he loved tractors even more!

BRUM! BRUM!
TRAC-TOR!

George loves tractors.
Everyone loves tractors!